Text copyright © 2001 by Rindert Kromhout
Illustrations © 2001 by Annemarie van Haeringen
English translation © 2007 by North-South Books Inc., New York

First published in the Netherlands by Uitgeverij Leopold Amsterdam,
under the title *Kleine Ezel en jarige Jakkie.*

Published in the United States, Great Britain, Canada, Australia, and New Zealand in 2007
by North-South Books Inc., an imprint of NordSüd Verlag AG, Zürich, Switzerland.

Distributed in the United States by North-South Books Inc., New York.
Library of Congress Cataloging-in-Publication Data is available.
A CIP catalogue record for this book is available from The British Library.

ISBN-13: 978-0-7358-2132-3 / ISBN-10: 0-7358-2132-1 (trade edition)
10 9 8 7 6 5 4 3 2 1

Printed in Belgium

By Rindert Kromhout

LITTLE DONKEY AND THE BIRTHDAY PRESENT

Illustrated by
Annemarie van Haeringen

Translated by
Marianne Martens

NorthSouth
BOOKS
New York/London

Jackie was having a birthday party. Little Donkey and his mama were going to buy him a present.

"Let's find something nice for Jackie," said Mama Donkey.

"Don't touch," said Ibis. "You break it, you buy it!"

Little Donkey looked around. What a lot of toys there were—far more than he had at home. Little Donkey spotted a kite with a long, long tail. "Let's get that!" he shouted.

Ibis wrapped up the kite, and Little Donkey and Mama Donkey
went home. What a beautiful kite! Little Donkey was sad that
it wasn't his birthday. He changed his mind about giving the kite
to Jackie. He'd rather keep it. He'd give him something else.
Little Donkey looked through his toys and found an old teddy
bear that he didn't play with anymore. "This would make a good
present for Jackie instead of the kite," he told Mama.

"What about the kite?"

"Oh, he won't like it. I'll just keep it," said Little Donkey.

Mama Donkey shook her head. "I don't think so. We bought that kite for Jackie. It's Jackie's birthday."

Sadly, Little Donkey put the old teddy bear back in the toy chest.

"Hop in your wagon, Little Donkey," said Mama Donkey.

"It's time to go! Where's the kite?"

"Lost it," said Little Donkey.

"You lost it?" asked Mama Donkey.

Unfortunately for Little Donkey, it didn't take her long to find the kite. Too bad—he thought he'd done a good job hiding it.

Little Donkey hopped into his wagon. Gently, he stroked the
present. "Mama," he said, "I don't want to go to Jackie's party.
I want to stay home. My tummy hurts."
"All right, then. We'll just go, give him the present, and then
we'll come straight home," said Mama Donkey. "Of course
you won't be able to have any cake if your tummy hurts."
Little Donkey certainly did like birthday cake.
Oh, but that kite—that beautiful kite with the long, long tail . . .

Suddenly, Little Donkey jumped out of
the wagon. He picked a big bunch of flowers.
"I'll give these to Jackie," he said.
"That's very sweet of you," said Mama. "But
you're still giving him the kite."

"Maybe he won't like it," said Little Donkey.

"And then he'll give it back to me."

"Maybe," said Mama Donkey with a smile.

"Happy birthday," said Mama Donkey.

"Did you bring me a present?" asked Jackie.

"Jackie, dear, you're not supposed to ask that," said Mama Yak
sternly. Slowly, Little Donkey took the present out of the wagon.
Jackie tore off the paper.

Jackie's eyes widened. "A kite!" he cried.
"Will you come fly it with me?"
Little Donkey was delighted to help. Together, they ran
up the mountain.

Little Donkey and the birthday boy flew the kite all afternoon.
Round and round the house they ran, up and down the
mountains. The kite flew higher and higher.
"Don't go too far," called Mama Yak.

The sun sank over the mountains, and the party was over.

"Come, Little Donkey, it's time to go home," said Mama Donkey.

"Not yet," said Little Donkey.

"No, time's up," said Mama Donkey. "It's time for a bath, and then straight to bed for you."

Quietly, Little Donkey sat in his wagon. High in the sky, he saw the kite still dancing in the wind.

"I think Jackie liked his kite," said Mama Donkey. "What a good
present you chose for your friend. Well done."

"Hmmm," said Little Donkey.

"Mama, when is my birthday?"

"Soon, my dear. Very soon."